This edition published by Parragon Books Ltd in 2014

Parragon Books Ltd
Chartist House
15–17 Trim Street
Bath BA1 1HA, UK
www.parragon.com

ISBN 978-1-4723-5190-6

Printed in China

Bubble Trouble

Bath • New York • Cologne • Melbourne • Delhi
Hong Kong • Shenzhen • Singapore • Amsterdam

Doc likes to play with her best friend Emmie and Emmie's little sister Alma. One of their favourite toys is a Bubble Monkey bubble blower.

The girls can't wait to have fun popping bubbles together!
Emmie puts Bubble Monkey on the picnic table and flips the switch.

Bubbles, bubbles everywhere!
Alma pops three bubbles, Emmie pops six
and Doc pops two bubbles at the same time!

Emmie's dog Rudi wants to pop bubbles, too. But Bubble Monkey stops working – she's run out of bubbles.

Alma fills up Bubble Monkey while Doc and Emmie chase after Rudi.
When she's done, she asks, "Is everyone ready?"

"Yes!" reply Doc and Emmie.

"One, two, three!" Alma flips the switch
… but there are no bubbles!

"Where are the bubbles?" asks Alma.
"I'll take a look and see if I can work out what's wrong," says Doc.

Doc takes Bubble Monkey to the clinic and brings her to life with the magic stethoscope.

"Hey, look!" Stuffy says. "Doc brought Bubble Monkey over to play."

"Sorry, Stuffy, but Bubble Monkey is here for a check-up," says Doc.

"What's a check-up?" Bubble Monkey asks, looking worried.

Stuffy explains that a check-up is when a doctor makes sure everything is working properly.

"It's nothing to worry about," Stuffy says, trying to comfort Bubble Monkey.

First, Doc runs some tests. She takes a feather from her bag and asks Bubble Monkey to blow it.
Bubble Monkey blows, but the feather barely moves.

"Let me try it!" says Stuffy.

Stuffy blows the feather right out of Doc's hand. It lands on Chilly's face!

"Achoo!" Chilly sneezes because the feather tickles his nose.

Next, Doc listens to Bubble Monkey's chest.

"Sounds like gloop is blocking your bubble pumper," she says.

"Are you having any other symptoms?"

"What are symptoms?" asks Bubble Monkey.

Doc explains that symptoms are things that hurt.

"It's your body's way of telling you that something is wrong."

"Well, I have a tummy ache," Bubble Monkey says.

"Can I give your tummy a little squeeze?" Doc asks.

She presses Bubble Monkey's stomach. Something shoots out and hits Stuffy in the chest.

"Ick!" says Stuffy.

Chilly tries to help Stuffy but they get stuck together!

"Weird," says Doc as she pulls them apart. "This is glue."

Doc heads back to Emmie's
garden to investigate.
"Alma, what did you put in
Bubble Monkey?" she asks.

Alma holds up the pink jar. "I used this," she says.

"Alma, the pink one is glue!" Emmie says. "The green one is the bubble soap!"

Doc rushes back to the clinic.
"I have a diagnosis!" she tells Bubble Monkey. "You have a bad case of Gunk-inside-atude."

"Toys need to be filled up right, just like people need to eat well," explains Doc.

Doc cleans out Bubble Monkey's tubes and fills her up with bubble soap.

"Thanks, Doc. I feel better!" Bubble Monkey cheers. "You're super-fantastic!"

"I love my job!" says Doc. "Now let's get you back to Emmie and Alma."

"I'm back!" Doc says. "And this time, I brought Bubble Monkey!"

"Did you fix her?" Alma asks.

"There's only one way to find out," says Doc.

Doc's Tips for Eating Well

- We should eat the right things to stay healthy and feel good.

- Eat a good breakfast each morning.

- Cut down the amount of sweets you eat.

- Eat plenty of healthy vegetables.

- Try to avoid eating fried, fatty foods.